Bad the Mystical Mutt

and the Loch Mess Mystery

McNicol & Jackson

THE LUNICORN PRESS

THE LUNICORN PRESS
Glasgow
Text © Lyn McNicol and Laura Cameron Jackson 2016
Illustrations © Laura Cameron Jackson 2016
All rights reserved

1

Printed by Martins the Printers, Berwick-upon-Tweed
Designed and typeset by Heather Macpherson at
Raspberry Creative Type
Set in 14.25 pt Gentium Book

British Library Cataloguing in Publication Data
A CIP catalogue record for this book is available from the British
Library

ISBN: 978-0-9929264-4-1

www.badgerthemysticalmutt.com
www.facebook.com/badgermutt
www.twitter.com/badgermutt

For Sir Robert Lauder of Quarrelwood

Prologue

Badger the Mystical Mutt opened the envelope nervously.

He pulled out a soggy letter and laid it carefully on the dashboard of the Wim-Wim. He peered at the smudged print and took another bite of toast. He stopped mid-munch as he began to make sense of the splodgy handwriting. It was from his relative in the Ring of Brodgar, who was extremely keen on setting him impossible tasks. *This calls for more toast*, thought Badger. His eyes widened as he read the letter again.

Dear Badger,
I have just spent the last few days with my good friend, Baroness Mess at Bigheart Castle in Scotland. She has had to leave the banks

of Loch Mess urgently to visit farthest-flung Siberia. The time has come for the elders of her breed to bestow to her the ancient Secrets of the Saur. You will be pleased to hear that she has our friends, the Narwhals, as her guides. She has left her son, Vincent, in charge at the Castle, looking after her two daughters, Vanessa and Violet.

You may wonder why I am contacting you, my most favourite Mystical Mutt.

The trouble is that Baroness Mess is worried about leaving her children home alone, at a time when the Loch and its land is growing more and more polluted. The Baroness is a dippydoppyloppydus, and mother to a family of dippydoppyloppydusses, known as "the Dippies". I'm sure you are aware of the legends surrounding Loch Mess: its mysteries and its monsters. The fact is that all of that is nonsense. The Dippies are not monsters, nor are they scary, and they need your help now. The Baroness is concerned that she has left them with a tricky challenge while she's away. The mess has got much messier and the clear-up may be too big for the children to handle on their own.

I have enclosed a map. The Wim-Wim will take you straight there, and on arrival, the map will show you the lay of the land and the murk of the Loch.

Yours in eternal gratitude
Captain Bravebark

Badger gulped. He did indeed know all about the legends surrounding Loch Mess and its scary monsters, which he had heard were as big as the Eiffel Tower with three huge humps. He believed they ate dogs like him for breakfast, and he feared his magic would not be powerful enough for this mission.

He picked up the envelope and unfolded the map, tracing his paw across an outline of a loch, a castle and a wood. But there was no mention of the monster. On the other side of the paper, he noticed another message from Captain Bravebark: a rhyme written in faint pencil. It read:

By human eye alone
Dippies cannot be seen.
There's nothing there more visible
than sloping banks of green.
On the first day of the fourth month
in any leaping year,
When a Dippy dips into the loch
there is plenty for them to fear.
The Loch was once a beauty
before the Big Folks came.
Then they dumped all of their rubbish

till it suited its new name.
Now the water is awash
with toxical pollution.
Can you go to messy Loch Mess
and seek a good solution?

Badger sighed: *Here's another fine mess you've got me into, Captain Bravebark.*

Then he remembered that he was Badger the Mystical Mutt. He crunched another slice of toast and sat up straight with purpose and pluck.

He punched some buttons on the Wim-Wim's navigation system and buckled up for take-off. Screens shot up to surround Badger in Perspex. The legs of his time-travelling machine began to move sideways like a crab, and a new leg sprouted from the middle, shaped like a giant pneumatic drill. A periscope popped out of the roof and a propeller started to whirr at its side.

Instead of shooting off into the air, the Wim-Wim burrowed deep into the ground below. Moments later, Badger zoomed through a subterranean tunnel. Soon he was submerged in the deepest, darkest and murkiest of waters. He covered his eyes in horror.

Suddenly, the Wim-Wim whooshed upwards and sped towards the surface.

Uh-oh! winced Badger, *I really hope I packed my water wings.*

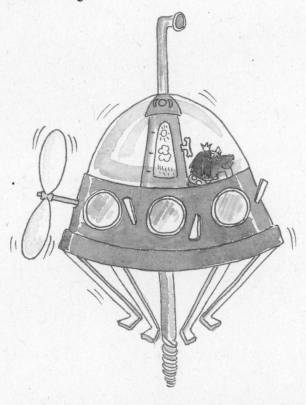

Chapter One

Splash! Gurgle! Hiss! At last, the Wim-Wim crashed through the surface of the water and hit fresh air with a burp. Badger clung on to the sides, his eyes still tightly shut.

The Wim-Wim bobbed along gently. Badger opened one eye nervously and spun around. He had a panoramic view of outside. Daylight shone through the portholes and billowing plastic bags floated past.

"Ahoy!" he yelled to the Wim-Wim, "I can see land, but I don't seem to be on it yet. Let's aim for that big rock ahead ... if we can make our way through the yuckiness."

He switched gear and zoomed his travelling machine towards the lump in the loch. He shoogled onto the land mass and shut down the engines. The Wim-Wim began to wobble. The land beneath him started to move and suddenly with a splash, the Wim-Wim was back in the water.

What on earth did I just land on? frowned Badger, peering out of the portholes.

Badger jumped in alarm as two enormous startled eyes with gigantic eyelashes appeared in front of him. Each eye filled a whole porthole of the Wim-Wim.

The creature tapped on the window and pointed to the lochside, motioning for Badger to follow.

Badger pushed the throttle on the Wim-Wim and headed for the shore. As he followed the strange colossal beast, he saw it was wearing a swimming cap patterned with poppies.

Surely, thought the Mystical Mutt, *anything wearing a flowery swimming cap like that has to be friendly!*

Badger bumped ashore in the Wim-Wim. He took a deep breath and opened the door. There, in front of him, was the creature, wearing a frilly swimming costume and what looked like a saddle of six rubber rings, three on each side. It was as big as a small island. It smiled at him. He grinned back warily.

"Hi," it said, "I'm Vanessa Mess. I'm a dippydoppyloppydus. Welcome to Loch Mess. What are you? A dog?"

Badger gulped, remembering the stories and hoped she wasn't too hungry.

Vanessa guffawed as she spotted his panic.

"Ha ha! I see you've heard the rumours! Don't worry, I don't eat dogs. Actually, I'm a vegetarian dippy, so you can relax."

Badger sighed with relief. This, of course, was one of the Baroness's daughters, and the reason for his mission. He was in the right place, on the right track, and soon he could sort everything out and get back to his higgledy-piggledy towers of toast

"Yes," said Badger. "Correct, I am a dog. I am indeed Badger the Mystical Mutt, and I've come to help."

"Help? Why? What's wrong?" replied Vanessa puzzled.

"I'll be delighted to hear that there is nothing wrong," said Badger, "but I was asked to come by a friend of your mum's. She's worried about you."

"Worried about me? Why? Mum's away at the moment and we are all home alone. Woohooo! I'm having a great time, or at least I *was* until recently.

I'm in the bad books with my brother and we've had a huge falling out."

"Why, what's happened?" asked Badger.

"When I came down to the Loch last week for my daily dip, I suddenly couldn't swim. I just seem to have forgotten how to do it!" frowned the dippydoppyloppydus.

Badger cocked his head to one side and scratched his ear.

"I am — or at least I *was* — a champion swimmer. I have trophies, medals and all sorts of certificates," she said proudly, pointing to the badges sewn onto her swimsuit. "My brother says I'm a show-off as I have plans — big plans — to swim the world. Apparently this Loch is linked to all sorts of subterranean channels, which connect to other countries around the

planet," Vanessa continued.

"Wow, really? Is it?" grinned Badger.

"Yes, I believe a map exists, but I've never seen it," she said.

"That's great, but why have you fallen out with your brother?" said Badger.

She leaned forward and whispered, "He's always trying to tell me, and my sister, Violet, what to do. Now, because Mum's away, his bossiness has got worse. Plus, I swam out of hours and he's never forgiven me."

"Out of hours? What's that then? A midnight dip?" asked Badger.

"No, quite the opposite. You know the stories about a monster here in this very Loch? That's me, you see. Can you believe it?" she giggled.

"You are actually the Loch Mess Monster?" said Badger nervously.

"It seems so," she chuckled. "But a dippy can only be seen in the water on the first day of the fourth month in any leap year. I got my years mixed up, more than once, and the Big Folk spotted me practising my lengths during those leap-year days a long time ago."

"So, it was more than a single sighting then? But why are you wearing the rubber rings? Aren't they going to make you even more obvious to the Big Folk?" asked Badger perplexed.

"Only if I swim on the forbidden day, but as I can't actually swim any more, the life belts are just to keep me afloat," said Vanessa glumly.

Badger shrugged his shoulders and said: "Vanessa, I still don't get it. *Why* can't you swim?"

"I don't know!" she shrieked. "Last week I could race along happily underwater, and today, I can't. My brother Vincent is insisting that I return to the Castle for my own safety, until I can remember how to swim again. But I cannot and will not leave my beloved Loch."

"Are you *grounded* until further notice?" Badger laughed at his own joke.

"Grounded? I'm usually in the water," said Vanessa bamboozled.

Badger shrugged and asked: "So, your brother has asked you to return to the Castle and you won't. Is that why you quarrelled?"

"I suppose so. He's really annoying. Just because Mum left him in charge, he thinks he knows best. But he also brought me the rubbers rings to keep me afloat, *and* freshly baked bread, so he's not *all* bad," she added.

Badger's ears pricked up at the mention of freshly baked bread. "Hmm," he said, "maybe your brother has your best interests at heart and you should return to the Castle as he asked."

"But he was horrible and said it was a good thing that I've forgotten how to swim. The Loch has become so messy recently, he said he doesn't want me submerged in the sludge," said Vanessa sadly.

Badger looked across the Loch and saw even more gunge, goo and garbage clogging up its surface.

"Right," said Badger gently, "let me go and see him and I'll let you know how I get on."

Vanessa nodded.

Badger looked at his map and headed towards Bigheart Castle, waving cheerio to his new friend, Vanessa, the *not-so-scary* monster of the deep.

Swimming is like riding a bicycle: surely you don't just forget how to do it? There's something fishy going on here, he thought, *and I will fathom it out!*

20

Chapter Two

In Niggledy-Nook Wood, Vanessa's sister, Violet, was coming to the end of her nightly beauty regime. The mud pack slabbered over her face was almost dry, and her tree-trunk rollers had curled all of her hair into long waves. Her bangles jangled as she added the finishing touches to her toenail painting with the latest colours of snail varnish. She dabbed her voluminous mouth with a touch of lip moss and put on her tie-dyed kaftan and favourite silver-birch sandals.

As night neared in the wood, Badger followed the path and picked his way through the litter. He felt the mist drifting in from the loch and sniffed the air. It was rich with the smoky aroma of patchouli incense. Lights flickered from lanterns hung

on branches. Ahead, he heard movement
and peeked out from behind a tree. His eyes
widened at the sight before him, where
a huge creature busied herself outside a
bright white yurt.

*Another dippydoppyloppydus! This must be
Vanessa's sister,* he thought.

He took a step forward to get a better
look, tripped over his own paws and fell
face-down in the bracken. Suddenly an
almighty *clank, clatter* and *clang* crashed into
the stillness of the evening. Badger covered

his ears and stumbled around as a tin-can alarm continued to rattle.

Violet reached for her night-vision goggles and spotted a black lump of fur prowling around her yurt.

"Who goes there?" she shouted sharply.

"It's only me, Badger the Mystical Mutt. I come in peace," answered Badger meekly.

"I'm not expecting any visitors. Show yourself at once!" she commanded.

Badger emerged from the shadows with his paws held over his head.

"Come closer," said the dippy, "and take two long steps to the left, if you please."

Badger did as he was told, but in doing so, he felt his legs slide away from him. With his paws flailing, he slipped into a gungy sludge until he was waist-high and unable to budge.

"Help!" he shouted.

"Stop mithering! You're fine. I have you just where I want you, in my mud bath. How's the temperature down there? Still nice and warm?" sniggered Violet.

Badger yelled out to his trusty neckerchief for some assistance: "'Chief, 'Chief, please heed my plea. Catch onto a branch and yank me free!"

But his neckerchief was also sodden with mud and the knot could not be undone.

"Who's this 'Chief you call to? Is he the Chieftain of the Clans? Have you come to seize Bigheart Castle from us while my mum's overseas?" demanded Violet.

"No, not at all. I told you, I come in peace. A friend of your mum's sent me. 'Chief is my magical neckerchief, who can *usually* help me out when asked." Badger frowned down at the red spotty cloth tied around his neck.

"What do you mean you were told to come? Why?" she asked, lighting a beacon and shining it onto the mud bath and Badger.

"She was worried about leaving you all home alone with a massive clearing-up task," said Badger, shielding his eyes from the glare of the light.

The dippy rolled her eyes and sighed.

"Right, hang on to this and I'll pull you out," she said pointing her broad swishy tail at him. Badger reached out his front paws, as he was still sinking deeper into the mud, and grabbed hold.

"One, two, three ... and up!" Violet ran forward, and soon Badger emerged from the sludge, covered in the stinkiest, wettest mud he had ever encountered.

As he shook himself dry, flecks of muck flew through the air and splattered every branch, pebble and blade of grass around.

"Here, let me dry your neckerchief," said Violet. She held it aloft and spun it round at the speed of light.

Badger stood mesmerized.

"There," she said, tying the neckerchief into a bandanna around Badger's head. "That's what we call a spin-dry in this neck of the woods."

Badger looked upwards warily.

"Now, the truth is, the only way I can possibly take you seriously is if you join me whilst I perform the rest of my ablutions for the night." She held out a hand, inviting Badger to take a seat while she flossed her fangs with a wire coat hanger. She put some powder on Badger's nose, then rubbed some knobbly slime onto his face and instructed him to sit back and relax.

"What have you put on my face?" asked Badger uneasily.

"It's just a slug mask. You've got some matted fur, and this will simply slither through and make it silky smooth," replied Violet sweetly.

26

Badger ran his paws over his face cautiously and flicked off several slugs.

"Er, no thank you very much, I'm quite happy with my face as it is," he said, quickly splashing his chin in a barrel of freezing cold water.

"I was just trying to help," said Violet, shaking some talc on his nose.

"And that's what I'm trying to do as well," said Badger sneezing. "Now, tell me about your sister Vanessa and your brother Vincent, and the terrible mess around here."

"Well, the mess is a big problem," she frowned. "Some Big Folk think they can just dump their rubbish here because it's Loch *Mess*. But it's becoming unbearable and the stink is awful."

Badger nodded and covered his snout with his paw. He looked around at the piled-up bin bags of rubbish. There were odd welly boots, tin cans and pans, old washing machines, wonky vacuums, boxes and brushes, and bubblegum goo. Strewn across

the woodland, the litter was everywhere.

"That's why I'm working on my beauty products: I have to find *some* elegance amidst all of this mess and ugliness," scowled Violet.

"I understand. It *is* shocking. And I may have a clean-up spell that will help. But, in the meantime, what's the story with your sister and your brother?"

Violet sighed heavily. "Vanessa and Vincent had a massive quarrel last week. Then Vanessa announced that she had forgotten how to swim and as Mum left Vincent in charge, he forbade my sister from going to the Loch again. He also told her that even when she can remember how to swim again, she can't visit the Loch until it's been cleaned. He's worried that she'll swallow something yucky and fall ill, as it's had so much rubbish dumped in it. He tried to make her stay at the Castle."

"Oh dear," said Badger

"Vanessa and swimming is like bread and butter: they go together," Violet continued, as Badger's tummy rumbled at the image of hot toast dripping with butter. "Like me, she's headstrong and refuses to take orders from our brother. So she stormed off in a huff and, as far as I know, has based herself at the Loch until Mum returns."

"Right, I'm off to see Vincent next and get his side of the story," said Badger, "but Violet, why are you out here in the woods and not in the warmth and luxury of Bigheart Castle?"

"I couldn't stand all the argy-bargy with Vincent and Vanessa. I needed some silence and I wanted to take the chance, while

Mum's away, to get back to nature and live simply on the land. I really want to make my organic potions and lotions, and this seemed like the best time to do it. Vincent calls me the 'Hippy Dippy'. But he's not happy that I'm also not at home," winced Violet.

Badger shook his head and strode off determinedly for the Castle. His nose may have been covered in talc, but it could still sniff out trouble.

He had come to sort out one mess and had stumbled into another mess entirely.

Chapter Three

Badger trampled across the heather towards the glow of the Castle. As he drew nearer, he heard a huge rumpus and racket. Bigheart Castle was ablaze with light and seemed to pulsate with noise and colour.

How very odd. I thought Vincent had been left in charge as custodian whilst his mum was away, he thought.

The Mystical Mutt approached the moat and stepped onto the drawbridge, which took him through the main gate and into a courtyard. He ducked as a wake of low-flying buzzards headed straight past him, then he moved on to the tall wooden doors of the Great Hall. He pushed them open and was stunned by a blast of light that swept towards him at great speed. A grand and glittering chandelier was festooned

with deer hanging upside down from it.
Their antlers were entwined and they
were swinging from it gleefully like a huge
pendulum.

"Whoaahhhhh!" they squealed.

As Badger stood open-mouthed, one of
the deer noticed him in the doorway and

shouted: "Hey, dude, welcome to the party!" Suddenly, he was grabbed from above and found himself swinging backwards and forwards with them across the Great Hall. They narrowly missed the fountain in the middle, where otters were jumping about to catch the spray of the cascading water. Badger looked on from above, utterly aghast. Statues wobbled with scurrying squirrels and dive-bombing birds. The hall was bustling with bedlam.

"Where's Vincent?" he shouted over the chaos.

"Who?" hollered one of the deer.

"Vincent!" shouted Badger, starting to feel a little bit sick with all the to-ing and fro-ing.

"Sorry, buddy, I've no idea," smiled the deer.

As the chandelier swung even faster, Badger let go and was flung headlong into a pair of velvet curtains. He slid down and landed with a bump on the floor, right next to the backing singers of the Highland Tiger Cat band.

A *boom-boom-boom* throbbed from a double-bass rhythm as a trombone blew *mwaah mwaaaah* in his ear. The Tiger Cats warbled, "Doo wop, doo wop, yeah yeah!" One of the cats twirled round to Badger and thrust a microphone in front of him.

"You're in the band," purred the singer, "so join in."

With a fixed smile, Badger uttered a few pitiful *doo wops* and weak *yeah yeahs* and then ran.

He slapped his paws against his ears.
The caterwauling was too much to bear.
He moved further inside to another large
medieval hall, where he discovered even
more pandemonium. A long table, heavy
with food, ran down the middle of the room
and more animals, in various states of
disarray, were sitting at or lay slumped over
it. In the corner, a red squirrel brandishing
a breadstick announced "On guard!" to a
grey squirrel wielding a long baguette.

Crumbs scattered into the air and
reminded Badger how very hungry he was.
His tummy rumbled. At the back of the
room, an elderly golden eagle sat in front
of a dusty grand piano slowly pecking out a
well-worn melody.

"Where's Vincent?" Badger asked one of
the hairy cattle.

"Who?" mooed the heifer.

"Vincent! The one in charge?" repeated
Badger.

The heifer shrugged and pointed over to
the gloomy golden eagle.

Badger walked over to the piano and lowered the lid on the keyboard. The eagle looked up with one eye and whistled.

"Sorry about that," apologized Badger, "but I'm looking for Vincent. Do you know where he is?"

The eagle spread out its magnificent wings, calmly lifted up the lid of the keyboard and snorted: "Can't help you there. I've never heard of him. Now beat it, kid, and let me play."

Badger took the hint and crept away.

In another corner, a barn owl was screaming wise-cracks in a quick-fire stand-up comedy routine. Its audience of merlins and ospreys was hooting with laughter and flapping its wings in mirth. Badger stood at the back and listened, looking for anyone who resembled Vanessa or Violet Mess.

You would think he'd stand out from the crowd alright, he thought. *Unless Vincent is a miniature dippydoppyloppydus.*

He moved on through a corridor and into a low-lit pantry. Here, a gang of Mohicaned

hedgehogs pogoed to a manic beat.

"Excuse me," asked Badger politely, tapping the lead singer on the back.

The hedgehog whirled round, raised its sunshades and scrunched its eyes at Badger.

"Mate, we're in the middle of our encore. This had better be good!"

"Sorry. Can you tell me where I might find Vincent, please?" asked Badger hopefully.

"Vincent? Vinnie? Vinda-who?" said the hedgehog, scratching his head, "Nope, don't know the geezer. You could try upstairs, because none of us lot *ever* go up there."

"That's great, thank you," said Badger turning towards the staircase. But as he did, a giant hula-hoop knocked him sideways and slid over his head. Instinctively, Badger

began to wiggle his hips to keep the hula-hoop from falling.

"Woohooo! You've been hoopla-ed," roared a bouncing hare, hopping towards him in a hurry. The hare was followed by a flurry of chattering bob-tailed bunnies. Badger leapt quickly out of the way, the hula-hoop fell to the ground, and the hare and the rabbits rushed on past.

Phew! he thought, *this is a mad house. I need to find this elusive Vincent or I won't get out of here alive.*

At last, he reached the bottom of the very wide staircase where all was quiet. But the first step was barricaded with a row of upright rolling pins.

As Badger lifted the first rolling pin out of the way, he heard a fox yell, "Watch out! We're in the middle of a bowling tournament here!" There was a rushing trundle behind him and he turned around to see a massive watermelon heading his way. As it crashed into him, he toppled to the ground with a heavy thud.

Birds fluttered around Badger's head as he lay there at the foot of the stairs, out cold.

Upstairs, in a darkened room, at the very top of the turret, a creature watched Badger drift into the Land of Nod.

Surrounded by a wall of silent TV screens with cameras trained to observe every detail of every room downstairs — even as far as Niggledy-Nook Wood and Violet's yurt, as well as the banks of Loch Mess where Vanessa was — Vincent watched.

Chapter Four

"Wake up, wake up! Are you alright?" heard Badger, as he came round to the short, sharp sting of freezing cold water on his snout.

He rubbed his eyes and sat up. A large beast in a floppy hat, white tunic and checked trousers towered above him, clutching a dripping mixing bowl. Badger looked closer and saw that the tunic bore a coat of arms with the royal 'Mess' emblem, and was covered in patches of floury white dust.

"Aha!" said Badger standing upright and holding out his paw, "you must be Vincent. I am delighted to finally meet you."

"Indeed, I am," smiled the dippydoppyloppydus warily, shaking Badger's paw. "I've been expecting you."

"Really?" asked Badger. "But I've only just arrived."

"Yes, but I've been watching you since you landed at the Loch. I have surveillance, you see. I believe you've already met my sisters."

"That is quite correct. I've met them both. I'm hoping you can shed some light on Vanessa's sudden inability to swim," Badger stated.

"There's plenty of time for all that. But first, let's get you dried and fed and I'll give you a proper tour of the Castle. You're a visitor to my home and therefore my honoured guest. I must make every effort to make you welcome. Follow me, if you please."

Vincent climbed the stairs to the Minstrel's Gallery overlooking the Great

Hall and invited Badger to take a seat. On the table in front of him a pile of hot toast oozed with butter. Badger's jowls began to dribble.

"How did you know that this is my most favourite snack ever?" asked Badger, eyeing the toast excitedly.

"I've done my research on you, the Mystical Mutt. I know all about you. Now, please, help yourself. It's freshly baked," offered Vincent.

To be mannerly, Badger took a few dainty bites, before speedily guzzling down the rest. He had never tasted such delicious toast before. He burped superbly and held his paw up to his mouth in apology.

"Who baked that? It's epic!" asked Badger.

"I did. Baking is a little hobby of mine," beamed Vincent.

"You should bake professionally," said Badger sincerely. Vincent blushed, dismissing the Mutt's compliment and asked: "Would you like a little nap now? If so, you can use one of the chambers on the next floor to put your head down for a bit."

The thought of a slumber filled Badger's heart with joy, but he knew he was there for a reason: he had to try and unravel the mystery of Vanessa and her swimming defect. And he had an uneasy feeling that somehow Vincent was behind it. He shook his head.

"Well then, let me introduce you to the Laird's Lug, if I may," Vincent suggested.

He handed Badger a funnel-shaped device.

"What's this?" asked Badger puzzled.

"It's an ear trumpet. In days past, the lords and ladies would retire up here to the gallery and be able to hear all the conversations going on in the Great Hall below."

"But isn't that a bit like snooping?" asked Badger.

"Well, I suppose it is, but it's great fun. If I know what everyone's saying then I can protect my family better."

"Hmm, I'm not so sure," said Badger raising his eyebrows, "But if you like the

sound of chatter, I have a spell to create your very own chatterbox. Would you like me to show you?"

"Go on," said Vincent intrigued.

Badger closed his eyes as sparkles of light appeared around him. He waved his paws over the funnel and uttered the magic words:

"Jabber, blabber and yakkety-yak,
Jumble together lots of chat.
Stuff the funnel with tattle and vox
And turn it into a chatterbox!"

Badger opened his eyes nervously. Nothing happened. Vincent looked at him suspiciously.

"Erm, it doesn't seem to have worked," said Badger bashfully.

All of a sudden the funnel rumbled and exploded into a thousand juddering, laughing bags, rather than boxes.

Chuckles, giggles, guffaws, titters, sniggers, chortles and side-splitting jocularity filled the gallery.

"Oh, maybe it sort of did!" giggled Vincent.

The hilarity was infectious: Vincent and the Mystical Mutt rolled around the floor, crying with laughter. At last, Badger managed to compose himself, and tried the spell again. This time, he concentrated much harder. The laughter bags disappeared one by one, replaced by a colourful box on the table beside them.

"Lift the lid, Vincent," Badger instructed.

Vincent gingerly prised open the
lid of the box, and at once the air was
crammed with babbling voices, murmured
conversations, tittle-tattle, gibberish and
mutterings.

Vincent covered his ears and quickly
crammed the lid fast shut.

"I think the Laird's Lug works fine for me, but thanks, Badger. This has been a jaw-droppingly eye-opening experience."

"We should always be careful of eavesdropping," said Badger wisely, "because that's when we hear things that we really shouldn't hear."

"I know that," agreed Vincent, "but how else can I protect my sisters? My mum has left me in charge to look after them, as well as clear up the mess in our grounds and down at the Loch."

"Well, I can help with a clean-up spell, as far as the mess goes," said Badger helpfully.

Vincent raised an eyebrow.

"Okay, I know that last spell didn't quite go to plan, but I assure you, I *will* get the clean-up one right."

Vincent raised another eyebrow.

"The matter we have to deal with right now is why do you have a houseful of party-goers, and why is the Castle in a mess?" asked Badger.

"I invited my wildlife pals to help me clean up, but they heard I was home alone and just thought they could have a great big party. The mess is now bigger than ever," sighed Vincent. "My mum will go mad if she gets home and sees this, and then discovers that Vanessa and Violet have both left. I don't know what to do."

"We'll get it sorted. Don't worry," said Badger hopefully.

Badger left Vincent for the night and headed back towards the Wim-Wim.

As he walked towards the Castle gates, he heard a series of whirring noises. He glanced behind him and spotted several cameras pointing right at him.

Chapter Five

It was almost daybreak when Badger returned to Niggledy-Nook Wood. Smoke seeped out of the top of Violet's yurt, and breakfast was already cooking on the fire.

Yum yum, yawned Badger, *time for another toastastic snack!*

"Well, look who it is! The interfering Badger," shouted Violet gaily as the Mutt approached.

"Good morning, Violet. I'm a dog who is *called* Badger, but I'm not *actually* a Badger," he replied respectfully.

"Whatever! What do you want now?"

"I went to see Vincent last night."

"And what has my brother got to say for himself then?" she harrumphed.

"Well, there was a bit of a party going on when I arrived," fidgeted Badger, sniffing the bread toasting. He drooled.

"A what?" shrieked Violet.

Badger's tummy rumbled noisily.

"Just wait till I get my hands on him," vowed Violet, "I can't believe he's had a houseful while Mum's away."

Badger stayed silent as he gratefully munched on several slices of hot-buttered toast. It was the same fantastic bread he'd had at the Castle. Inside, his mind was racing with the most sensitive way to tell Violet and Vanessa that their brother actually needed their help.

Meanwhile, Vincent was watching from his control tower in the turret back at Bigheart Castle, through a camera trained on his sister's yurt in Niggledy-Nook Wood. He was sorry he'd told Badger that he didn't know what to do. He needed to maintain an air of control and some authority, otherwise his sisters would never respect him.

In the cold light of day, he could see now that Badger was a nuisance that he could do without. He could not allow this so-called "magical mutt" to scupper his plans for being "in charge" of Bigheart. He sent an urgent plea to his pesky buzzard pals.

With a full tummy, and none the wiser, Badger set off to meet Vanessa on the banks of Loch Mess.

As he trampled across the bracken, he had the unnerving feeling of being followed. He noticed a shadow on the ground. He stopped. The shadow stopped too. He moved

forward, the shadow moved forward. It followed his every step. He looked up. To his horror, he saw a swarm of buzzards hovering above him. Before he could run for cover, the boss of the buzzards shouted an order:

"Talons at the ready! One, two, three ... and swoop!"

Immediately, they dived. Their long, powerful claws snatched his fur and lifted him up. The buzzards soared swiftly into the air and across the Loch, with Badger

dangling helplessly below them, heading towards a crannog in the middle of the water. They flew lower and dropped him onto the shore with a noisy bump.

Badger yelped, rubbed his bruised behind and looked around him. There was a sign saying *Welcome to Dog Island*, but not much else.

He checked around the bushes and bracken, but couldn't spot any cameras.

He peered into the sky, but the buzzards had buzzed off.

Badger sat down and looked out across the Loch. It was too wide and too deep to attempt a doggie paddle, but he had to get a message to Vanessa. He laid his head back on the bush and tried to think of a plan.

All he could hear were the waves lapping gently against the shore. He sighed and rubbed his eyes.

"I could always fly," he yawned, "but it would take a bit of effort." His eyelids grew heavy. He looked down to his neckerchief and started to mutter a spell:

"'Chief, Chief, please fly away,
And speak to Vanessa without delay.
Tell her she must come alone,
and join me as my chaperone."

But before Badger could finish, his eyes closed. The ebb and flow of the waves had lulled him into a deep sleep.

Badger's red-and-white polka-dot neckerchief fidgeted, then unfurled from his neck, twirled around his head and soared over the Loch.

The Mystical Mutt was dreaming happily of a higgledy-piggledy tower of toast when a noisy commotion jolted him from his slumber. He awoke to see the unmistakable dome of the Wim-Wim on the horizon, with Vanessa waterskiing behind it. He waved.

"Ahoy, landlubber!" screamed Vanessa. The Wim-Wim zoomed towards him and bumped ashore. Vanessa followed and was catapulted straight into the bushes, still on her water skis.

Badger's neckerchief settled quietly back around his neck. He patted the red-and-white polka dots and whispered respectfully: "Thank you for being awesome and bringing Vanessa here. Sorry I fell asleep." 'Chief ruffled with pride.

Vanessa emerged from the bush, a little dishevelled, but bursting with enthusiasm.

"You made it!" shouted Badger.

"I did indeed. I haven't had so much fun in ages," she roared. "Now, why am I here, and how can I help?"

"We're going on a trip to find out why you can't swim," smiled Badger, rummaging in the Wim-Wim. He handed her an air tank with a bendy tube attached to a mouthpiece "But first, there's something I need to do."

Badger closed his eyes as sparkles of light appeared around him. He whispered the words of the signal-jamming spell he'd been practising and concentrated very hard:

Cut the surveillance and jam all the panels.
Remove infra-red and block every channel.
No on-screen display but lots of white noise.

Create interference that really annoys."

Sparks gathered in the air crackling with interference and sped across the Loch towards the Castle.

"There!" said Badger looking very pleased with himself. "That should do the trick whilst we are away."

"Do what trick?" asked a bemused Vanessa.

"Never mind. It's just a spell I've been practising. Now, let's get rid of those rubber rings."

"I'm putting my complete trust in you Badger, because if I don't have these floats, you do know, I can't swim," screamed Vanessa, shrugging off the rubber rings.

"All will become clear shortly. Now, hook up the air tank and grab on to the Wim-Wim. We're off to meet a friend of mine," said Badger, leaping into his time-travelling machine.

Back at Bigheart Castle, Vincent was having technical issues with his CCTV equipment.

In Niggledy-Nook Wood, Violet was looking fondly at old photo albums; at pictures of Vanessa with her swimming trophies and Vincent with his prize cupcakes. She pulled her kaftan closer. The nights were drawing in, and she was keen to return to the Castle soon.

Meanwhile, Badger in his trusty Wim-Wim, with Vanessa clinging on behind, sank slowly into the murky depths of the Loch, studying the map Captain Bravebark had sent him.

Chapter Six

Bloop, bloop, sounded the Wim-Wim with its lights on full-beam. It dropped deeper and deeper before tilting sharply to the left, then came to an abrupt stop at the bottom of a flume-like tunnel.

"Hold on, Vanessa," Badger mimed at the porthole, as he engaged the jet-propelled turbo-charged engines on the Wim-Wim. The dippydoppyloppydus gripped the periscope and closed her eyes.

Suddenly, the water churned and the Wim-Wim blasted upwards through the channel. As they neared the top, Badger saw a light in the distance. He gave a confident thumbs-up to Vanessa to signal that they were nearly there. Landing lights shone like lasers through the water. The Wim-Wim rose upwards through a pool into a dark

cavern. Badger pressed the hydrodynamic friction lever on the dashboard and opened the vents on the ballast tanks to reverse and park up poolside.

He pointed to Vanessa that she was free to remove her air tank and mouthpiece.

All was eerily quiet and dark.

Badger touched his neckerchief, and

immediately all the white polka dots on the red cloth lit up like a torch to lead the way. He and Vanessa clambered onto the rocks.

"Wow, where are we?" asked Vanessa excitedly.

Before Badger could answer, a series of clicks, squeals and trills resonated throughout the cave. Badger shone his neckerchief in the direction of the sound. It was coming from the pool. The surface rippled faster and faster, as a spotlight underneath grew bigger and brighter.

Suddenly, a colossal crash burst out of the water.

Vanessa shrieked and squashed Badger in a terrified squeeze as a whale-like mammal with a dazzling horn emerged.

Badger disentangled himself from Vanessa's grasp and stepped forward.

"There she is," he said calmly, "My favourite water feature: the Narwhal."

"What's a Narwhal?" asked Vanessa hesitantly.

"A Narwhal is the unicorn of the sea ... or in this case, loch. She is, I assure you, our

friend," said Badger crouching down at the pool edge and stretching out his paw.

"Yes, yes, it's been far too long," trilled the Narwhal promptly, holding out her fins to greet the Mystical Mutt. Tell me how I can help and I will do my best."

Badger looked at Vanessa and back at the Narwhal.

"My friend has lost her ability to swim. She was, until very recently, a champion swimmer. It's a complete mystery and I'm baffled. Can you scan her and see if you can find the answer, please?"

"Of course," said the Narwhal, "Close your eyes, my dear."

Vanessa shut her eyes tightly and stood very still, as the Narwhal slowly traced her spiralled tusk around the dippydoppyloppydus's aura. All of a sudden, lasers shot out of the Narwhal's horn to form a rainbow-coloured shimmering force field around Vanessa.

Badger held his breath as the Narwhal concentrated.

After a few moments, the Narwhal's horn withdrew and the multi-coloured neon-lit spectacle crackled and faded.

"As I thought, Badger; your friend has been bewitched."

Vanessa gasped.

"Bewitched? But surely that involves magic and a spell? There's nobody around Loch Mess with such powers that I know of," said Badger in disbelief.

The Narwhal nodded and nudged Vanessa kindly. "You must look closer to home, my dear. Who would wish to disable your swimming prowess so badly that they would call in help from others?"

Vanessa looked at Badger, her eyes filling with tears.

"Surely Vincent wouldn't go this far to take my passion away from me?" she sniffled.

Badger tried to put his arms around her, but her body was so big, he could only reach her knees.

"Rumour has it that buzzards possess powers of an enchanted nature and will do almost anything for a slice of fish pie," suggested the Narwhal.

Badger remembered his abduction to Dog Island and had a flashback to the party at the Castle when he had had to dodge a load of low-flying buzzards.

"Do you want to know how to reverse the spell so that you can swim again?" asked the Narwhal.

"It doesn't matter anymore," sighed Vanessa, "Not now that I know how much my brother despises me."

"Ah but, my dear, can't you see that it matters *even more* now?" said the Narwhal gently. "You must not hide your light so that others can shine. Sometimes the very thing you need is right in front of your eyes, in clear sight. The antidote, my dearest, is nearby. It can be found right next door to the poison. And it is always within your power to change situations. That is all." The Narwhal uttered a whispered rhyme into Badger's ear and swam off.

Vanessa looked at Badger in bewilderment.

"What does that mean?" she wailed.

"I don't know, but I have a feeling we're about to find out," said Badger mystified as he climbed back into the safety of his waiting Wim-Wim. Vanessa followed him wearily, as he practised a much-needed spell for their arrival back on Dog Island.

Back at the lochside, more trucks trundled up and dumped their rubbish into the water.

Chapter Seven

Violet tutted and tsked.

Enough is enough, she decided. *I must see my brother now and find out more about this so-called party he had. Mum could return any day, and she'll go mad if Vincent has made an even bigger mess.*

She walked down to the Loch in the hope of catching sight of Vanessa, but the waters were completely still with a cloak of fog hanging above.

She trekked back towards the Castle, angrily kicking empty tin cans out of her way.

As Violet crossed the drawbridge, she surveyed the surrounding chaos.

In the distance, she heard the rumble and trundle of another Big Folk truck.

Uh-oh! she gulped. She peered through the mist towards the water and gasped. The

lights of the lorry cast an eerie light over the lochside. She watched in horror as three burly Big Folk tipped a giant skip full of junk onto the grass, then drove off quickly.

Violet shook her head sadly and wrung her hands. *How could they ever hope to stop this dumping when the Big Folk didn't even know they were there?*

She plodded on through the courtyard. When she entered the Great Hall, she found, to her shock, all sorts of unwanted guests asleep on the plush sofas and armchairs. A magnificent red deer lounged on her favourite chaise longue, alongside a lopsided coronet and several Highland Tiger Cats. Violet grimaced as she knew the coronet to be a cherished family heirloom. A squirrel scurried past her hiccupping, while another casually tossed monkey nut shells onto the vintage Persian rug.

As she moved through the corridors, she found yet more muddle and disarray. She shook a dishevelled hedgehog awake to ask if he had seen Vincent.

"You're the second person to ask us that very same question in as many days. We still don't know *who* he is, or *where* he is, but like we told the other fella, you could try upstairs. No one ever goes

there." The hedgehog pointed to the wide stairwell.

"Thank you very much," said Violet haughtily, "I think I can find my *own* staircase in my *own* house."

"Oooooooooh! Sorry for trying to help," said the hedgehog huffily, returning to his slumber.

Violet climbed the stairs, knowing only too well she would find her brother at the very top of the Castle.

Even as a child, and especially when he'd been naughty, she thought, *Vincent had always disappeared to his hidey-hole in the tower turret, where he had his very own wood-burning stove. There he would bake for days, creating new breads and cakes.*

Violet reached the top and slammed open the door to the turret. The distinctive aroma of freshly baked cake filled her nostrils immediately. All was in darkness, but for scratchy electric interference on surrounding screens. The only other sound she could hear was the snivelling of her brother.

"Now there, there," said Violet, running to comfort him. "What is the matter, Vincent? You can tell me. I'm your sister. Did your cake sink in the middle?"

When he saw his younger sister, Vincent immediately fainted into her arms. Violet rummaged in her pocket for a tissue, and brushed the flour dust from his forehead. He came round within seconds and looked up at his sister with fear in his eyes.

He bit down on his lip and wailed: "It's all gone wrong. My screens won't work. I've lost control. I can't take charge if I can't monitor everything that's going on. I can't be everywhere, so these screens are my eyes. I've been blinded, Violet, blinded!"

"Don't talk such nonsense, Vincent! What do you mean *screens?* Mum has never needed all this technology. She manages to do a good job of running the family and home. You can see me, can't you? So you're definitely *not* blinded."

Vincent looked up at his sister hopefully.

"Now, I have some questions for you," said his sister sternly. "Who are all those creatures downstairs, and what has happened to Operation Clean-up? You were supposed to have all the mess removed before Mum gets back. It's worse than ever downstairs. And I just saw another truck dump its load outside."

Vincent shook his head and wrung his hands.

"No, I'm not falling for this!" said Violet firmly. "You can't just shrug your shoulders and make it all go away. I need answers, and you can start by explaining exactly why Vanessa is suddenly unable to swim."

"I only meant to teach her a lesson," Vincent confessed, "just to stop her from swimming in the Loch. It's not safe: it's becoming more and more polluted every day. But she wouldn't listen ..."

"So what did you do?" asked Violet uneasily.

Vincent cringed: "I asked the buzzards to share an anti-swim spell. I mixed up the concoction, put it in her favourite lemon drizzle cake and she ate it."

"Right, take me to Vanessa now!" she commanded.

Vincent rose reluctantly and headed towards the door.

"Haven't you forgotten something, Vincent?" his sister asked, pointing to the stove. Vincent grabbed his oven mitts and pulled the perfect cake out of the oven.

"I'll take this with us as a gift for Vanessa," he smiled weakly.

"I think Vanessa might have had quite enough of your baking when she finds out what you've done. Oh, and one other thing, before we go," smiled Violet sweetly, "Do you have a Tannoy in here?"

"Erm, yes," replied Vincent, pointing to a small upright microphone on his desk. "What do you need it for?"

"I need to make a public address immediately," said his sister, clearing her throat.

She pressed the button on the Tannoy and announced in an extremely authoritative voice: "The Party is officially *over!* Would all guests please leave Bigheart Castle *now!* And *never* return!"

Downstairs, all the creatures shook as the blast of Violet's powerful tones made it very clear that they had to leave the premises at once.

"Now get a grip, Vincent!"

When Vincent and Violet arrived at the banks of the Loch, all they found was Vanessa's saddle of lifebelts bobbing lifelessly on the surface.

"Oh no!" yelled Vincent, throwing down his beautifully crafted cake. "What have I done?"

Chapter Eight

Vanessa donned her mouthpiece and air tank and clung on to the back of Badger's Wim-Wim. They began to wend their way back towards Dog Island.

She shrieked with delight as they swooshed down the flume and out into the murky depths of the Loch once more.

Badger felt something tug at the back of the Wim-Wim. He looked around and saw Vanessa in conversation with a three-spined stickleback fish.

"Come on," mimed Badger through the glass to the dippydoppyloppydus. "We have to hurry. There's no time to stop and chat."

Vanessa waved off her stickleback friend and grinned. She swam to the windscreen, and excitedly held up two tickets to the Algae Arcade to see the Electric Eel Band.

She tilted her head and fluttered her eyelashes and pleaded with Badger to go, pointing to bright blue flashes of light flickering through the plankton. Badger shrugged. He turned the Wim-Wim around and followed the lights.

Eventually, they arrived at the Algae Arcade. Badger remained, watching in the Wim-Wim, as the Arcade was underwater and he could only hold his breath for so long. They took their places amongst the gathering of loch life: eels, pike, trout, salmon, Arctic char and the minnows ... and waited. The atmosphere was electric as all eyes focused on the stage.

Suddenly the bladderwort curtain rose, and a hush befell the awaiting audience. Badger switched on the Wim-Wim's headlights to create a spotlight. Vanessa squealed with delight as the Electric Eel Band took the stage and began to play. Sparks flew as the band played *plinkety-plonk*

muzak. The brass section swung smoothly
from left to right and had the audience all
swishing and swaying. Vanessa sashayed
her tail and bobbed her head to the rhythm
as Badger bopped around the Wim-Wim
smiling.

Suddenly, Vanessa spluttered. Badger
looked anxiously at her from behind the
glass.

"Her air tank!" he gasped. "It's running out."
But before Badger could jump to her
rescue, a trumpeter eel had leapt off the
stage and was by her side. He blew his
trumpet calmly into her jaws
and gave her the kiss of life.
"That should give you
enough breath to get
to where you need
to be," winked the
eel.
Vanessa
blushed and
thanked her trumpeter
saviour.
"There's more than you
think in that trumpet blow. The air velocity
is higher and the vibration will give you
part of what you need for your antidote,"
said the eel knowingly.

"How do you know about that?" asked
Vanessa.

"We know more than you think. We are
friends and we're electric. Now save your

breath and get back to Dog Island. The minnows will guide you. They know all the shortcuts to avoid all the dumped debris and litter," rasped the eel, slithering back onto the stage.

Vanessa tapped the glass on the Wim-Wim and gestured for Badger to leave the Algae Arcade and head back to Dog Island. A shoal of minnows waited for them at the exit.

Badger in his Wim-Wim, with Vanessa hanging on at the back, followed the minnows all the way to the gravel and peat beach of the crannog.

The Mutt berthed his vessel ashore and tied it up. Vanessa heaved off her air tank and flung away her mouthpiece. She was back on dry land.

"Now what?" she asked Badger as he stepped out of the Wim-Wim.

"We follow," said Badger spotting an overexcited otter that was jumping up and down and waving at them impatiently.

They ran after the otter as sun broke through the branches overhead. In the

shadows of the trees, a patch of bright-red berries shone like scarlet jewels in the dew. The sky around them was filled with sharp-scented blossom. The otter jabbed its paw at the centre of the cluster and ran off.

Badger sniffed the air and remembered the spell from earlier. He held Vanessa's massive hand, closed his eyes and whispered:

"Untangle the seeds of this heartless spell
With forget-me-nots and speedwell,
Rosemary spikes and sweet honeysuckle.
Mix it all up and regain Nessa's chuckle."

Sparkles of light appeared around Badger's head. The blossom swayed in the light breeze, the dew glistened and the overhead branches quivered. The spell to bring back Vanessa's ability to swim was done. But would it work?

Chapter Nine

"Stop screaming!" Vincent shouted to his sister.

By the banks of Loch Mess, Violet was inconsolable.

"I gave Vanessa the lifebelts when she forgot how to swim. They were supposed to keep her afloat," he yelled.

Violet wailed louder. Vincent gulped guiltily.

The fact that the rubber rings were there, on the shore, without Vanessa, was *Not A Good Sign* at all.

"Right!" said Vincent bracing himself. "Leave this to me."

He removed his hat and limbered up with ten quick star jumps.

"Leave this to you?" screamed Violet. "You got her into this mess, so you had better get her out of it!"

Vincent dived into the Loch.

Violet slumped on a rock and flicked her tail in anguish.

Vincent had only swum a few hundred yards before he sensed that he was not alone in the water. He looked over his shoulder and saw flashes of blue sparks following him. The Electric Eel Band was in hot pursuit, with the trumpeter leading the way. He tried to swim faster, but they soon had him trapped. They hissed and spat, then the horn player slithered up to meet him eye to eye.

"So, you're the brother; the one that did the deal with the buzzards to stop our friend Vanessa from swimming?"

"No, I'm here to help Vanessa, to find her and bring her home," blubbed Vincent.

"So you say, so you say," buzzed the eel, glaring at him. "But I don't believe you!"

"Look, let me go free, and you can have all the fish pies you want, served up to you daily," Vincent whimpered.

"Isn't that what you promised the buzzards for giving you the spell? You have stopped our friend Vanessa from doing the thing she loves most: swimming! Okay, let's ring him in, guys," shouted the leader eel.

Vincent felt his body being wrapped tightly by the seething eels.

"That's what happens when you mess with our friend," sniggered the leader eel, slinking around him. Underneath the water, Vincent was bound from toe to neck in a

swaddle of electric eels. He couldn't move his body at all.

From the banks of Loch Mess, Violet spied her brother's head peeking out of the water and became even more hysterical. She shook off her kaftan and headed for the water to rescue him.

But just as she was about to take a step into the murky depths, a periscope popped up in the water in front of her.

Chapter Ten

Badger's Wim-Wim emerged from the Loch and as it settled onto the bank, he jumped out.

"Violet, what are you doing here?" asked Badger surprised.

"I came down here, hoping to find Vanessa, but when we found her lifebelts, Vincent jumped into the water to save her. But look at him now!" said Violet in a panic, pointing out to the middle of the Loch. Then she spotted her sister emerge from the water and ran to embrace her.

Vanessa could swim again.

Badger's spell had actually worked.

"Vanessa, you're okay. Thank goodness. You're swimming!" cried Violet.

"I am indeed! It's fantastic, and all thanks to Badger, who managed to reverse a certain anti-swim spell," winked Vanessa.

"When Vincent told me what he'd done to stop you from swimming, we both dashed down here. As soon as we saw your rubber rings, he swam off immediately to rescue you," said her sister.

Vanessa harrumphed.

Badger looked behind him. He had to hide his smirk when he saw Vincent's head poking above the surface of the Loch.

"Can you help him?" asked Violet.

Vanessa looked crest-fallen. Badger comforted her and said: "I know you're angry with Vincent, but he's still your brother, and he's in a bit of a pickle right now."

"Vanessa, Vincent explained to me why he tried to stop you swimming. He was only trying to protect you from the pollution in the Loch," added Violet.

"Maybe Vincent is desperate to prove he can be responsible while your mum's away. He's the one who was left in charge, after all," continued Badger.

"I know Vincent can be infuriating, Vanessa, but I've been thinking a lot about this. I wonder if, next to you and all your achievements, he feels a bit left out. Mum's always talking about your latest trophies," Violet suggested carefully.

"That's claptrap. Mum is extremely proud of Vincent's flapjacks and his apple turnovers," stressed Vanessa.

"But what does *Vincent* believe?" asked Badger, looking at Vincent's hatless head and then back at Vanessa, who seemed to be thinking very hard.

"Vanessa," pleaded Violet, "whatever he thought then or thinks now, the minute he discovered you were in danger, he did everything he could to rescue you."

"Right," said Vanessa determinedly. "I'll speak to the eels. They'll listen to me and release him."

She slipped into the water and swam towards Vincent.

"She's an eel-whisperer," said Violet casually to Badger as he looked on speechless.

From the shore, Badger and Violet could see Vanessa with her brother. She dived underneath the water for minutes and reappeared smiling. She cradled Vincent's head in her hands and pulled him towards the shore.

When they arrived, Violet ran to wrap Vincent in her kaftan.

"Thank you," she whispered to Vanessa.

"Vanessa," said Vincent, "I'm so, so sorry. I've behaved terribly. How can I make it up to you?"

"Well," Vanessa snorted, "by telling me the spell you cast to stop me from swimming?"

Vincent flinched.

"You've got to understand, Vanessa, I thought Mum liked you and Violet more than me. You've always been so brilliant with your swimming, and Violet's been so great with her organic beauty products that I just felt side-lined, and that my love of baking was somehow silly," moaned Vincent frantically.

"You do tend to show off a lot, Vanessa," added Violet gently.

"Yes, but you're always so hippy-dippy with your lotions and potions, Violet," pouted Vanessa.

"You just wouldn't listen when I asked you to stop swimming," Vincent said.

"First of all, that is so not true about Mum favouring us over you. She's mad about your choux pastry and sends your recipes across the world. But I don't understand why you would forbid me from the doing the thing that I love most! That's just nasty ... and taking advantage of Mum being away," scowled Vanessa.

"I did it for your own safety. The Loch has become more and more polluted. There are poisonous gases swirling around now, created by the Big Folk dumping all their waste. Swimming could make you seriously ill," shrugged Vincent.

Badger raised his paw to interrupt, "I can possibly help with a detoxification spell to purify the water in the Loch again."

Vincent laughed scornfully and said: "With all due respect, Badger, I've already seen how your spells can go wrong."

"The antidote reversal spell worked okay, as I can swim again," said Vanessa, sticking up for her new hero, Badger.

"Either way," reminded Violet, "this squabbling isn't getting us anywhere. Mum is due back soon, and she left *you* in charge of mess removal, Vincent."

"Me? Why is it always all down to me? I have one sister who disobeyed my requests and recklessly went off to swim, and I have another who decided to leave me alone in the Castle and disappeared to live in a yurt."

Vanessa and Violet looked at each other shame-faced.

"It's true. He has a point," said Violet.

"Maybe," admitted Vanessa, "but Vincent, you still haven't revealed the anti-swim spell to me. Tell me that and I will come up to the Castle and help with the clear-up."

Vincent sighed and recited the spell:
"*With barnacle suckers and tangleweed tuggers,*
Two thorns of the haw and merriment huggers,
Whenever you swim on the Loch of the Mess
Nostrils will quiver and fins will depress
Just tiny titbits of this fine lemon drizzle
And every air bubble will just be a fizzle."

"Every air bubble will just be a fizzle?" screamed Vanessa incredulously.

"Well, maybe I didn't really think through the consequences. But that's why I saddled you with the rubber rings. I can't begin to tell you how I felt when I saw your lifebelts at the lochside. I was terrified something awful had happened to you. I was distraught. I can't imagine you not being here."

Vincent looked earnestly at his sister.

"How on earth did you get me to eat that hideous concoction?" asked Vanessa ignoring his excuses.

"Ah, well, I made a cake, of course. It was hidden in the sumptuous sponge of your favourite lemon drizzle," admitted Vincent nervously.

"I remember that cake," said Vanessa licking her lips. "It *was* delicious. Why couldn't you just have given me the cake and left the other ingredients out?"

Vincent hung his head in shame, "Because I wanted to stop you from swimming in this pollution. And the truth is, I wanted to stop you from leaving Loch Mess to swim the world. You're always going on about this supposed map that shows the tunnels linking all the subterranean channels and how, when you find it, you'll be able to jaunt across the world and leave us behind. If this mysterious map ever appears, I'd miss you."

"Oh, Vincent," said Vanessa softening. She hugged him warmly. "Please don't miss me when I travel the globe. I won't be away forever, only for a bit. Why didn't you tell me you felt like this?"

Vincent smiled sheepishly. "I didn't really know this was how I felt until I got squeezed to a wheeze by your friends, the eels. It put things into perspective."

"All of this can be sorted out," whispered Vanessa, holding his hand.

Badger raised his eyes.

"Really?" said Vincent, "While Mum's been away, I've done a pretty rubbish job of being in charge: both of you have left home; I've put one sister in danger; hosted an unplanned party; the Castle is in a state; the grounds are still messy; there's more and more being dumped every day; and the Loch is now even more polluted. What do you think Mum will make of that? She'll banish me when she returns ... *if* she ever returns. I suppose I should pack my bags now," he added wistfully.

Just then, a bird dropped a letter at their feet. It was from the Baroness. She was finally coming home.

Chapter Eleven

It was mayhem at Bigheart Castle. Everyone helped. Every trace of Vincent's party had been removed. The beds were stripped, the floors were mopped and the china was washed. Vases were emptied and swilled out, mats were beaten, sofas were vacuumed, curtains were opened, tables were polished, ornaments were feather-dusted and the kitchen was scrubbed. The deer, the squirrels, the otters, the Mohicaned hedgehogs, the bob-tailed bunnies, the hares, the foxes, the birds, the heifers and the Highland Tiger Cats had all been recruited to help with the clean-up.

Badger, Vanessa, Vincent and Violet huddled around the big old kitchen table. Badger wiped away the crumbs from yet another toastastic snack.

For once, the siblings, along with their wildlife pals, had pulled together to make the Castle chambers as tidy, clean and mess-free as possible.

However, the major mess and what to do about *outside* still hung over them all like a very bad smell.

"The problem we have," groaned Vanessa, "is that the Big Folk don't know we exist as we're invisible to them."

"Except in the water, on the first day of the fourth month in any leap year!" added Vincent.

"Yes, thanks for reminding me of my slip-ups all those years ago, Vincent," frowned Vanessa.

"But how does that work?" asked Badger. "Why are you invisible to them, apart from on that one day in the water?"

"Aha," revealed Vanessa, "as you know I am an eel-whisperer, and I made a pact a long, long time ago that the eels would use their electric current to create a force field of invisibility around Loch Mess, Bigheart Castle and our grounds."

Badger nodded, very impressed.

"So because the Big Folk don't know *we* are here, they think no one can see *them* plonking all their junk on our beautiful land," explained Violet.

Badger scratched his chin thoughtfully and suggested, "What if Vincent took all his cameras and equipment, put them outside the force field and put up some signs?"

The others looked at him doubtfully.

He continued excitedly, "It's a deterrent. If the Big Folk think that they are on camera and that there will be a penalty for treating your land as a rubbish tip, then they are less likely to dump their trash."

"Ooooh!" said Violet clapping her hands together, "What an excellent idea!"

"One of the signs could say LITTER LOUTS WILL BE PROPERLY BOOTED," said Vanessa.

Badger smiled. "I think you mean *prosecuted*, Vanessa."

"Another sign could say, IF YOU DUMP DOWN HERE, YOU HAVE PLENTY TO FEAR," added Vincent.

"And one could say, SMILE! YOU'RE ON CAMERA," beamed Violet, "Or BEWARE OF LOW-FLYING SCONES."

"Speaking of which, Vincent, I presume you *are* baking some scones for Mum's return?" asked Vanessa, fetching a slab of butter and a bag of flour.

"Are you sure that's a good idea?" asked Vincent apprehensively.

"Why would making scones ever be anything other than a very good idea? Now, we don't have much time, so get to it and rattle those bowls and spoons. Violet and I will get on with making the signs," ordered his sister.

Vincent needed no further encouragement. He flicked his floppy hat and hurried off happily.

Badger's neckerchief twitched. He jumped to his feet and announced shiftily: "I must pop out for a bit. I need to check on a few p-mails and that the Wim-Wim is safely anchored."

"Off you go then," declared the sisters, "but be sure to be back before dusk as we know Mum will want to welcome you officially when she returns."

Badger bowed to them both and ran outside.

"Now then 'Chief," he muttered, looking fondly down at his red-and-white polka-dotted neckerchief. "There must be something we can do to clear up this mess for the Messes before their mum returns."

He closed his eyes and sparkles of light twinkled around his nose. He had remembered a rare tidy-up spell from centuries ago. He uttered the magic rhyme carefully:

"De-clutter this junk and return to senders.
Deliver the litter to all the offenders.
Make this land green and a true scenic beauty.
As nature's patrollers, it is more than our duty.
The Loch of the Mess must be purified,
Purged of the poison it has so far survived.
Filter pollution and let it all shimmer,
For it must be safe for a champion swimmer."

Suddenly broken washing machines, curtain rails, planks of wood, cardboard boxes, cracked plant pots, black bin bags, crooked tables, sodden mattresses, chunky televisions and all sorts whirled into the air and flew off across Loch Mess to back and front gardens and driveways throughout the land.

Badger looked proudly at the scene in front of him. He could see grass: the landscape was green and completely uncluttered. In the distance, the Loch glittered its gratitude, cleansed at last of all contamination.

"That's a badgical-magical job extremely well done. I really am quite brilliant when I put my mind to it," he grinned. His neckerchief tugged. "But I'd be nothing without you, of course, 'Chief," added Badger hastily.

At the Loch, the Baroness, flanked by a fleet of Narwhals, spotted land. She was almost home.

In houses across the country, Big Folk opened their doors in horror to find junk tipped up onto their patios, clogging up their ponds and messing up their gardens. Some of them recognized their old furniture and appliances, but others ranted and raved at the downright trespass and complete disregard for their properties. One of the Big Folk's houses was swamped by a slurry of cascading cartons and discarded pizza packaging, whilst another was hemmed in by washing machines and wellies.

Badger the Mystical Mutt made his way to the lochside to greet the Baroness, who appeared wearing a bright yellow diamante sou'wester and a floral twin-set.

"Ahoy!" shouted the Mystical Mutt, "Good to have you back."

The Baroness clambered ashore, and shook herself dry.

"You must be Badger the Mystical Mutt. You made it then? Have I missed much?"

"Not at all," fibbed Badger. "It's all been very quiet here. I really don't know why you were worried. Your children have handled everything wonderfully in your absence."

The Baroness raised a suspicious eyebrow.

"Look," said Badger, waving his paw at the banks of greenery, "even the mess has gone."

"Well, my word!" gasped the Baroness, "It's beautiful. Captain Bravebark did say you were capable of the mightiest of magic, but *this* is a miracle."

Badger beamed in delight.

The Baroness took a package from her waterproof cummerbund and rolled out a scroll to show him.

"This is the Secret of the Saur," she whispered.

Badger nodded knowingly and escorted the revered dippydoppyloppydus up to the Castle.

Chapter Twelve

At the Castle gates, Vanessa and Violet had seen them coming and were ready with open arms to welcome their mum back home.

After the Baroness had scoffed at least four floury scones filled with raspberry jam and cream, she sat back and sighed.

"Ah, that's better! There are no such delicacies in furthest-flung Siberia. I've so missed honest home baking. Talking of which, where *is* that son of mine?"

Vanessa gulped. Violet looked troubled. And Badger snaffled another scone.

The Baroness sighed and pulled the tassel on the bell wire.

Within seconds, Vincent appeared, covered in flour.

"Mum, you're home at last!" he trembled. "Apologies for my appearance, I've been baking."

"Glad to hear it, Vincent," said the Baroness, embracing her son. "Now, you and I have some catching up to do. Follow me, if you will, into my office."

Vincent swallowed, looked at his sisters and nodded to his packed luggage at the door. He followed his mum into her study with his fingers crossed.

Inside the study, all was quiet. The fire crackled in the hearth and there was an air of majesty around the room. The Baroness invited her son to take a seat in the big comfy armchair facing her desk and poured him a cup of tea.

"Now, exactly what has happened while I've been away?" she asked.

Vincent cringed.

Back in the kitchen, Badger endured another slug mask from Violet and explained how he had managed to get rid of all the rubbish.

Vanessa giggled as Badger winced. The mud of his face pack had hardened on his fur. He crinkled his snout and screwed up his eyes.

"Well," said Vanessa gleefully, "I think this happy event calls for balloons, banners and party poppers."

"Does my face pack really need that sort of celebration?" asked Badger flummoxed.

Vanessa and Violet tittered. "As much as your slug mask, is a sight to behold, Badger, the razzamatazz is for Mum's return home and to celebrate the successful clean-up," they replied, placing party poppers around the room.

Vanessa blew up the balloons and stuck them to the wooden beams overhead. Violet draped a HAPPY WHATEVER banner over

the mantelpiece, and produced a tray of Vincent's canapés from the oven.

Soon, the study door creaked open and The Baroness and Vincent emerged.

His mother placed a ceremonial gold chain around his neck.

Vanessa, Violet and Badger clapped with glee.

"Vincent is now the Mayor of Mess," declared the Baroness. "My visit to the elders in furthest-flung Siberia was very special. Our species is becoming extinct. We are the last of the Scottish dippies, and so they wanted to bestow certain traditions to me before they leave this earth forever. With that, they explained that my eldest son should take on the mantle of Mayor, which comes with enormous responsibility, of course."

Vincent looked awkward and hung his head.

"Shape up, boy! You should be pleased, not shame-faced," scolded the Baroness.

"I'm overwhelmed, but I just don't feel I deserve it, after my recent behaviour," said Vincent.

"Poppycock!" roared the Baroness looking around the room. "Do any of us here feel that young Vincent is not worthy of this honour?"

Vanessa, Violet and even Badger cheered.

"And there's more," boomed the Baroness.

The others gathered around her wide-eyed.

"I was summoned to receive the Secrets of the Saur, and that is exactly what I have returned with," she said, holding up an ancient scroll.

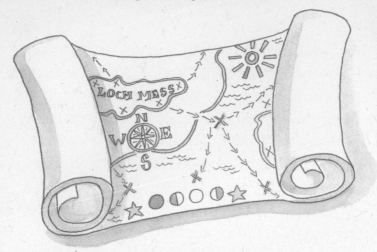

They all gasped.

"On this very parchment is a map. That it exists at all is a miracle. That we should have it in our family is an honour indeed. It has been sought for centuries to no avail. Now, our elders have gifted it to us. I present to you: the Secrets of the Saur!"

The Baroness spread the map out on the kitchen table. Her family and Badger pored over it zealously.

"Here," pointed the Baroness, "are the routes for all of the world's subterranean channels linking Loch Mess to every continent on this earth. Every sea, ocean, river, lake and loch is connected."

"Wow!" squealed Vanessa. "This means I can plan my trip and actually swim the world!"

"Indeed you can, my dear. You can pass invisibly from country to country, and no one will ever know you've been there," said her mother proudly. "Violet, you can continue to make your lotions and potions but now, thanks to this map, you'll be able to import herbs like sage and saffron from the Mediterranean, basil from India and even manuka oils from New Zealand."

"Double wow!" echoed Violet. "That's awesome! It means I can finally make the elusive *Crème de Mess* I've been dreaming of."

Vincent crumpled. He couldn't see how this was of any interest to him.

"And Vincent," added the Baroness turning towards her son, "I have a proposal for you, which will make good use of this map too."

Vincent perked up and listened avidly as his mother continued.

"You are a master baker. It's time we exported your wares around the world. This map gives us the perfect opportunity to do that. So, tomorrow I'm contacting those wretched buzzards for a quote on some building work. I'd like, with your permission of course, to install an industrial kitchen in the pantry. Are you ready to create your baking masterpieces and cater internationally?"

Vincent nodded enthusiastically.

"Then, let's do it," agreed the Baroness. "It's time to put the produce of Bigheart Castle — and my talented children — on the map"

Everyone applauded and Vincent smiled. For the first time in his life, he felt useful.

The nibbles from the oven were transformed into a banquet, and they all feasted and enjoyed a happy family reunion.

As Vanessa retired to her bedroom, her feet itched and her fins fidgeted excitedly about her adventures ahead.

Violet decided that it was not a night for the yurt and climbed the stairs to her old chamber and dreamt of patchouli from the Philippines.

Vincent crept into his turret and started work on new recipes for flat-bread fabulousness and cake extravaganzas.

The next morning as Vanessa came downstairs, her mother called her into her study.

She entered nervously, worried that now her mother was going to chastise her for dis-obeying her brother.

"My darling girl," said her mother kindly, "it looks like you have a big trip to plan and we are all going to miss you. However, dreams should always be pursued, and we all want to support you."

Vanessa looked at her mum excitedly.

"So, I want to give you this," said the Baroness handing her a sonic sonar hydrophone.

"The destination is set for Bigheart Castle, with lots of stop-off points along the way, including every corner of the globe," she smiled. "It's just to make sure you know where home is, sweetheart, and so you can always stay in touch"

Vanessa burst into tears.

"Why are you sad, my girl?" asked the Baroness.

"I'm not sad. I'm crying with joy," wept Vanessa.

"Well, that's good, isn't it? Now pull yourself together and let's have some breakfast. Vincent has made waffles and maple syrup for you," offered the Baroness.

In the kitchen, Badger, Violet and Vincent sat with smiles as big as Cheshire cats.

The dippies presented their sister with two parcels.

"But it's not my birthday or even Christmas. Why do I have presents?" asked Vanessa.

"Because it's a *Whatever Day*, that's all," said Vincent shyly.

Vanessa opened the first parcel from Violet and found a brand-new flowery swimming cap with built-in headphones.

"That's so you can listen to the latest tunes from that annoying Electric Eel Band whenever you want," said Violet.

Vanessa flung her arms around her sister and gave her a great big kiss on her cheek.

She opened the second parcel, from Vincent, to find a sponge cake in the shape of her favourite swimming cap, complete with edible flowers.

"Amazing!" gasped Vanessa, pinching at some of the icing, "Yum yum!"

"And for you, Badger," announced the Baroness, "because you gave up your time to come here and help my family, we have a gift for you too."

Badger jolted in his chair. He had not expected this.

"We have installed a top-of-the-range, ten-slice toaster in the Wim-Wim for you," the Baroness smiled.

Badger quivered in his chair.

"And that's not all!" she continued. "As a token of our affection, and a thank you for your invaluable assistance, here is a loaf of Vincent's finest bread and a slab of butter, along with a jar of Violet's famous slug mask."

Badger spun around in his chair excitedly, his nose twitching. He was desperate to get back to the Wim-Wim.

"Now," said the Baroness, "let's go and wave Vanessa off on her epic adventure."

They strolled down to the lochside as Vanessa put on her sonic sonar hydrophone and headphones. She hugged them all and promised to send postcards.

The Electric Eel Band put on a massive show of sparkly blue radiance to light her way, while a lone trumpeter stood on Dog Island and played a fantastic fanfare.

With a copy of the map tucked safely under her swimming cap, she set off across the Loch for her trip of a lifetime.

Vanessa was finally free to swim again, and she was aiming for the world.

The following week, Vincent organized his first Mayor's Open Day at Bigheart Castle. The invited guests included the deer, the squirrels, the otters, the Mohicaned hedgehogs, the bob-tailed bunnies, the hares, the foxes, the birds, the heifers and the Highland Tiger Cats, who drooled over Vincent's tantalizing tray bakes.

As promised, the Baroness had installed an industrial kitchen in the pantry with super-duper electric mixers, whisks and ovens. Vincent baked to order. Catering demands arrived from all over the globe, and he was soon run off his feet.

Violet ordered heaps of herbs from around the world and began to craft her exclusive *Crème de Mess.*

All was well with the Messes of Mess.

Badger returned to his anchored Wim-Wim with his loaf of bread and slab of butter.

As he scoured the instruction manual and figured out the settings on his top-of-the-range toaster, he thought: *Maybe now I can sit back, enjoy my toast and relax.*

As the first ten slices of bread popped out of the toaster, Badger looked out of the port hole and admired the beauty of the land. He was happy. But as his job was done, it was time now to return home to his garden, next to the crack in the fence, in the Lane.

Epilogue

At Bigheart Castle, The Baroness chuckled as she looked at the pictures on Vanessa's many postcards from her visits around the world.

One was of her smiling and clinging onto the torch-bearing arm of the Statue of Liberty in New York. Another was of her swinging from one of the branches of

the Hanging Gardens of Babylon. Another showed her shoulder to shoulder with the Colossus of Rhodes. In the most recent one, she was climbing the Great Pyramid of Giza.

Her mother was happy that her eldest daughter was, at last, fulfilling her dream. In each postcard there was no mistaking Vanessa's happy grin.

Violet teamed up with the famous

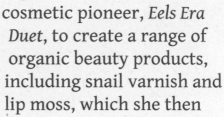

cosmetic pioneer, *Eels Era Duet*, to create a range of organic beauty products, including snail varnish and lip moss, which she then franchised to several continents. Her *Crème de Mess* potion was an immediate hit.

Vincent was constantly praised for his good works as Mayor of Loch Mess and became very generous with charitable donations.

His bakery became famous all over the world. His range of cinnamon-dusted and honey-infused oatcakes gained the Royal

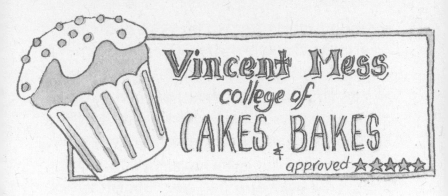

Seal of Approval, and he opened the Vincent Mess College of Cakes and Bakes.

Meanwhile, the Baroness developed a keen interest in marine biology and wrote a thesis on her endangered friends, the Narwhals.

After a year of travelling, Vanessa grew homesick. She returned to the banks of Loch Mess and set up a swimming school. Her classes were extremely popular and she soon created a synchronized swimming team with the minnows. They spent many hours in the Loch choreographing their routines to the rhythmic beat of the Electric Eel Band.

The signs remained in place at Bigheart and around the Loch. They acted as a superb deterrent for Big Folk dumping, particularly the IF YOU DUMP DOWN HERE, YOU HAVE PLENTY TO FEAR sign, as one Big Folk reported a sighting of a strange beast on the Loch on the first day of April in the following leap year. None of the Big Folk ever dumped any rubbish ever again.

The land blossomed and the Loch radiated health and well-being. It even received an award for Environmental Lustre from the Big Folk Ministry of Sheen.

The Dippydoppyloppydusses would thrive in Loch Mess for centuries to come.

Back in Badger's garden, next to the crack in the fence, the Mystical Mutt caught sight of something hitting a puddle with a definite plop: an urgent air-mail delivery addressed to *Badger the Mystical Mutt*.